Ex-Library: Friends of
Lake County Public Library

THE TALE OF PETER RABBIT

Grosset & Dunlap

3 3113 01961 5402

Text copyright © 2000 by Frederick Warne & Co. Illustrations from *The World of Peter Rabbit and Friends*™
animated television and video series, a TV Cartoons Ltd production for Frederick Warne & Co.,
copyright © 1992 by Frederick Warne & Co. All rights reserved. Published by Grosset & Dunlap,
a division of Penguin Putnam Books for Young Readers, New York. GROSSET & DUNLAP is a trademark
of Grosset & Dunlap, Inc. Published simultaneously in Canada. Printed in the U.S.A.

Frederick Warne & Co. is the owner of all rights, copyrights and trademarks
in the Beatrix Potter character names and illustrations.

Library of Congress Cataloging-in-Publication Data is available.

ISBN 0-448-42089-9   A B C D E F G H I J

THE TALE OF PETER RABBIT

From the authorized animated series
based on the original tales
BY BEATRIX POTTER™

Grosset & Dunlap • New York

LAKE COUNTY PUBLIC LIBRARY

Once upon a time there were four little rabbits, and their names were Flopsy, Mopsy, Cotton-tail, and Peter. They lived with their mother in a sand bank, underneath the root of a very big fir tree.

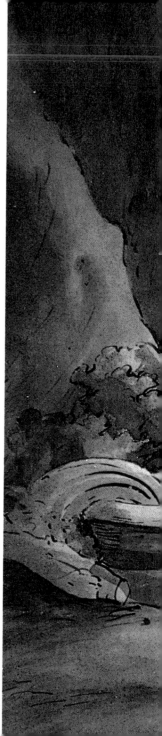

"Now, my dears," said Mrs. Rabbit one morning, "you may go into the fields, or down the lane, but don't go into Mr. McGregor's garden. Your father had an accident there—he was put into a pie by Mrs. McGregor." Then Mrs. Rabbit took her basket and umbrella and went through the wood to the baker.

Flopsy, Mopsy, and Cotton-tail, who were
good little bunnies, went down the lane to
gather blackberries.

But Peter, who was very naughty, ran straightaway towards Mr. McGregor's garden…

...and squeezed under the gate!

First he ate some lettuces and some French beans;
then he ate some radishes.

Peter ate so many radishes that he began to feel rather sick. He went to look for some parsley.

But who do you think he should meet
around the end of a cucumber frame?

"Oh help!" gasped Peter. "It's Mr. McGregor!"

Mr. McGregor was planting out young cabbages, but he jumped up and ran after Peter, shouting, "Stop, thief!"

Peter was most dreadfully frightened; he rushed
all over the garden, for he had forgotten the way
back to the gate. He lost his shoes and ran faster
on all fours.

Indeed, Peter might have gotten away altogether if he had not run into a gooseberry net.

"Hurry, Peter, hurry," urged some friendly sparrows.

"It's no use," sobbed Peter, trying to struggle free.
"My brass buttons are all caught up."

Mr. McGregor came up with a sieve, which he intended to pop upon Peter. But Peter wriggled free, leaving his jacket behind him.

Peter rushed into the toolshed
and jumped into a watering can.
It would have been a beautiful
thing to hide in if it had not
had so much water in it.

Mr. McGregor was quite sure that Peter was somewhere in the toolshed, perhaps hidden underneath a flower pot. He began to turn them over carefully, looking under each.

Presently, Peter sneezed, "Kertyschoo!" and Mr. McGregor was after him in no time. Peter jumped out of a window and ran off. Mr. McGregor was tired of running after Peter. He went back to his work.

Now Peter was quite lost. He found a door in a wall; but it was locked and there was no room for a fat little rabbit to squeeze underneath.

An old mouse was running in and out over the stone
doorstep, carrying peas to her family. Peter asked her
the way to the gate, but she had such a large pea in her
mouth that she could not answer. Peter began to cry.

Then he tried to find his way straight across the garden, but he became more and more puzzled. Peter came to a pond where a white cat was staring at some goldfish. He crept away quietly; he had been warned about cats by his cousin, Benjamin Bunny.

Peter went back towards the toolshed. But suddenly, quite close to him, he heard the noise of a hoe—*scr-r-itch, scratch, scratch, scritch*. He came out, and climbed upon a wheelbarrow, and peeped over. The first thing he saw was Mr. McGregor hoeing onions. His back was turned towards Peter, and beyond him was the gate!

Peter ran as fast as he could, slipped underneath the gate, and was safe at last in the wood outside the garden.

Mr. McGregor hung up the little jacket and the shoes for a scarecrow to frighten the blackbirds.

Peter never stopped running or looked behind him till he got home to the big fir tree. His mother wondered what he had done with his coat and shoes.

I am sorry to say that Peter was not very well
during the evening. His mother put him to bed
and made some camomile tea; and she gave a
dose of it to Peter!

But Flopsy, Mopsy, and Cotton-tail had bread
and milk and blackberries for supper.

Ex-Library: Friends of
Lake County Public Library